For Evelyn Rose, Lena Grace,
Celeste Rosa Lakshmi in the north and Wanga in the south

B.N.

For Maman and Baba

M.V.

For thousands of years, people have been telling stories.
From this rich global heritage, we can find stories that are
strikingly similar but also different. *One Story, Many Voices*
explores well-known stories from all over the world.
For teacher resources and more information, visit
www.tinyowl.co.uk

Copyright © Tiny Owl Publishing 2018
Text © Beverley Naidoo 2018
Illustrations © Marjan Vafaeian 2018

First published in the UK in 2018 by
Tiny Owl Publishing, London
www.tinyowl.co.uk

A catalogue record for this book is available from the British Library.

ISBN 978-1-910328-29-3

Printed in Malta

Beverley Naidoo

Cinderella of the Nile

Marjan Vafaeian

TINY OWL

One Story, Many Voices

There are many 'Cinderella' tales around the world but this is one of the earliest. The 'Egyptian Cinderella' legend was first written down more than 2000 years ago by the Greek historian Strabo and, before him, Herodotus. They say a girl called Rhodopis ("rosy-cheeked" in Greek) was captured in Greece and taken as a slave to Egypt in North Africa. Herodotus tells us of her friendship with the great storyteller Aesop.

I still have my childhood copy of *The Blue Fairy Book* with its 'Cinderella and The Little Glass Slipper'. It's the version with the fairy godmother and the pumpkin, first written in French by Charles Perrault in 1697. A small label inside the cover shows that it was bought for me at the 'People's Bookshop' in Johannesburg, the city where I grew up. The book was published in London in 1949 and my copy must have travelled soon afterwards on a boat to South Africa.

Books and stories are wonderful ways of 'mind travel'. My *Blue Fairy Book* didn't say where Cinderella lived but the illustrations suggested somewhere in Europe long ago. I was a child living 6000 miles away but I could still imagine being her. That's why stories are powerful. They take us into other people's lives.

However, at the time, my mind was still travelling inside a bubble. It was a 'European bubble' in which most of the ideas, pictures and words were shaped in Europe. Today, there are many more books and stories that allow children to hear voices from around the world and that encourage them to move beyond a single story.

Of course, tales change when they are told and retold. That is the freedom of the storyteller. I hope that you will use the same freedom to make your own versions too...

Beverley Naidoo

Long, long ago when pirates freely roamed the seas around Greece, a beautiful baby girl was born in a village to the north. She had eyes like sapphires and fine red curls. The happy parents, who had waited many years for this child, called her 'Rhodopis' because her cheeks were so rosy.

Rhodopis was a kind child who loved milking the goats and helping to make cheese. She collected water from the well, fed the chickens and did everything her parents asked with a smile.

"You are our treasure!" they said.

However, other villagers whispered that her greatest treasure
was her hair, the colour of the finest sunset.

As Rhodopis grew, word of her unusual beauty spread over the
mountains. Her parents thought they were safe living far away from
the sea but news of their red-haired daughter reached a band of pirates.
A girl like this could be sold for a fat bag of silver coins.

So it was that one afternoon, a bandit silently watched Rhodopis
herd the family's goats up the mountain. She sang sweetly.

Hurry up, my pretty ones,

no wolves are near.

I'll chase them away

with my stick here!

When Rhodopis drew near, the bandit leaped
out and grabbed her.

"Mama! Papa!" she cried, but the bleating
of the goats drowned her voice.

For days and nights, Rhodopis stumbled up and down mountain paths, bound by a rope. At the end of the fifth night, she felt her legs would give way. But just as the sun began to rise, she saw a sheet of silver stretching ahead as far as the sky on the other side.

The bandit grinned. "You're going over the sea, my pretty one. If my eyes see true, that ship there comes just for you!"

Down by the sea, a bright blue kingfisher landed on a rock beside Rhodopis
and cocked its head. Quickly, she plucked a few strands of her hair.
The kingfisher neatly grasped them from her hand.
Through her tears, she sang softly.

Little bird, you can fly,

you are free!

Tell my parents

you saw me by the sea.

My village lies

in those mountains there.

You'll hear their cries.

Please give them my hair!

She had barely finished her song when the bandit seized her and waded
into the water, with Rhodopis like a sack over one shoulder. By the time
she could turn her head, there was no sign of the little kingfisher.

Night and day, the boat rolled and swayed. Rhodopis stayed curled like
a mouse between two chests. Then one night, a storm sent huge waves
crashing over everyone and she thought they would all drown.

Yet when the morning star arrived, the sea was calm. Rhodopis was silent as the pirates cheered and she heard them shout, "Land!" A pirate shook her. "Soon we arrive in Samos! Get up, get up!" They were sailing towards a piece of land surrounded by sea.

Rhodopis was sold to the highest bidder and, by midday, trembled before the man who had bought her. Too scared to look up, she heard him say, "She is as beautiful as I was told." Her duties were to serve him and tend to his wife's garden. It was light work and Rhodopis soon learned to do it well. However, her heart remained heavy.

Now, there was one field slave who
was allowed inside the house. Rhodopis often found
the master sitting and listening to him. His name was Aesop and he was
a storyteller. Aesop reminded Rhodopis of her father who loved telling
stories about wolves, bears and other animals that lived in the mountains.

One day, entering the room, Rhodopis overheard her master complain,
"My red-haired girl is beautiful but she doesn't smile." Embarrassed, she quickly
left. Later, while watering a rose bush in the courtyard, she became aware of Aesop
watching her. He pointed to a tree. "You have a friend," he said. Rhodopis looked up
and saw a tiny owl. "Oh, Little Grey One!" she whispered and,
for the first time in many weeks, she smiled.

From then on, whenever she wasn't busy, Rhodopis would search outside for Aesop. She helped him feed the chickens, milk the goats and make cheese. She told him about her goats and the little grey owl that lived under the roof of her parents' house and Aesop taught her about the wildlife of the island.

He also told her stories that made her smile. However, when she returned to the master's house, so did her sadness.

This went on for some time until one day the master became very angry. "You have an easy life in my household yet you will not smile for me!" he shouted. Even Aesop could not calm him. Soon afterwards, the master announced that he had sold his red-haired slave to a merchant who was travelling to the city of Naukratis in Egypt.

Poor Rhodopis ran out of the house to find Aesop. Although her friend could not stop her being taken away, he told her a fable...

An oak tree boasted that it was stronger
than the reeds along the bank of a river.

That night, the mighty tree was uprooted
in a storm and crashed to earth.

The next morning, the reeds were still standing...
"We know how to bend," they whispered to the tree.

Night and day, wild waves battered the boat sailing to Egypt. Huddled among other frightened young captives, Rhodopis remembered Aesop and sang to herself. At last, the boat entered a wide river with tall green reeds on each side. As the shaking and shuddering stopped, a sailor cried out, "The great Nile welcomes us! Give thanks!"

Blow wind, blow,
I promise to be strong.
Watch me bend, not break,
with my little song!

The next day, a slave master herded the captives off the boat at the port of Naukratis and led them to a busy marketplace. Never had Rhodopis seen so many people. Suddenly, she was snatched from the crowd and placed in front of an old man with a woolly white beard.

So it was that the Greek merchant Charaxos bought Rhodopis and took her into his household. After hearing how she had been stolen from her parents in the north of Greece, he treated her more like a daughter than a slave. He insisted that she eat with him and bought her new clothes. He even gave her a little house with a garden running down to the Nile.

Now this angered his Egyptian servants, especially three sisters who lived in a hut made of mud and reeds. Old Charaxos slept a lot and they were mean to Rhodopis behind his back.

Rhodopis did everything to be friendly but they rubbed dirt into clothes she had washed and dropped sand into food she had prepared. "So, you think you're better than us!" They laughed. Rhodopis never said anything but did the work again as she hummed to herself...

Blow wind, blow,
Watch me bend, not break!

Remembering Aesop, she made friends with the ginger cat and pet monkey that lived with Charaxos. Down by the river, she talked with Hoopoe and Hippo who loved to play splashing games while Cat and Monkey played hide and seek among the reeds.

They made Rhodopis laugh, helping her to forget her sadness. After washing the clothes, she would sing and dance for her animal friends, swaying this way and that...

With my little song
I promise to be strong!

One afternoon, Charaxos woke up early from a nap. When he didn't find Rhodopis in the house, he walked down to the river and there he found her dancing barefoot. He watched, hidden behind a palm tree.

A few days later, Charaxos presented Rhodopis with a pair of rose-red slippers embroidered with gold thread. "Oh thank you," she whispered. "Never before have I seen such beautiful slippers!"

Soon afterwards, the Pharaoh sent out an invitation to all his subjects to attend a feast at his palace in Memphis. Rumours spread that he was looking for a bride. The three sisters were excited. They would dress in their finest clothes and he would notice one of them!

Of course they said nothing to Rhodopis or their master who rarely left the house. Instead, they made up a story. "Our parents are ill and need us urgently," they cried with false tears. Charaxos agreed they should go immediately and Rhodopis offered to do their chores.

Every day, Rhodopis carried a basket of clothes to the river.
She removed her new slippers so as not to wet them. One day, she
was bent over the water when a vast winged shadow swooped over her.

She looked up to see Horus the Falcon soaring upwards with a rose-red slipper gripped in his sharp talons. "For pity's sake, please bring my slipper back!" she begged. But the falcon-god of the sky was gone. Her animal friends tried to comfort her as she cried hot tears.

Horus flew south along the valley of the Nile to the great palace at Memphis. Pharaoh Amasis was tired of the feasting. Indeed, some of his subjects had begun to quarrel. He was listening to their complaints when a small rose-red slipper fell from the sky into his hand. He glimpsed the falcon sweeping away. "Horus has sent me a sign!" Amasis declared. "The owner of this slipper must be found!"

Messengers were sent east, west, north and south. The three sisters arrived at the palace just in time to see them disappearing in their chariots. How furious they were to learn that the feast had ended and the Pharaoh himself was about to leave! When they heard about the search for the owner of a small rose-red slipper with gold thread, they looked in disbelief at each other but said nothing.

The royal musicians played their instruments as the royal barge set sail with Pharoah Amasis. Word spread quickly. Day after day, young women from villages along the Nile hurried to its banks for their chance to try on the slipper. But none had a foot small and slender enough.

As the royal barge approached, Rhodopis held back to watch from behind some reeds. How amazed she was to see the Pharaoh and her rose-red slipper in the hands of a royal servant! The three sisters jostled with others to try it on but, once again, no one's foot fit the tiny shoe.

"This is the slipper of a child!" the sisters complained loudly.

Just then Rhodopis heard a bird cry on the other side of the reeds.
A bright blue kingfisher had accidentally caught itself in a net.
Stretching forward, she gently untangled its wings and set it free.
It reminded her of another kingfisher, on another shore, long ago.

The Pharoah saw this and was curious. Why had this red-haired girl not come forward with the others? He signalled to his servant to take the slipper to her. As her foot slid in neatly, Rhodopis laughed shyly.

Pharoah Amasis descended from his barge to greet Rhodopis. "Horus chose well. You are kind as well as beautiful," he said.

The three sisters cried out, "Great Pharaoh, she's just a slave! She's not even Egyptian!" Waving them away, Amasis declared that Rhodopis would be his Queen.

It is said that Rhodopis and Charaxos shed tears as they said goodbye. Did she ever see her parents, or Aesop, again? We don't know. But they surely remained in her heart and legend says that Rhodopis and her Pharaoh lived happily together for the rest of their lives.